The Bamboo Cutter & the Moon Maiden

A Silverleaf Press Book

Silverleaf Press Books are available exclusively
through Independent Publishers Group.

For details write or telephone
Independent Publishers Group, 814 North Franklin St.
Chicago, IL 60610, (312) 337-0747

Silverleaf Press is a wholly owned subsidiary of Leatherwood Press LLC.

Leatherwood Press LLC
8160 South Highland Drive
Sandy, Utah 84093
www.leatherwoodpress.com

Teresa Pierce Williston's text was originally published in
Japanese Fairy Tales, Second Series, New York City: Rand McNally & Co.; Chicago, 1911.

Illustrations Copyright © 2006 by Dilleen Marsh

ISBN 1-933317-39-6

The
Bamboo Cutter &
the Moon Maiden

タケおよび日本の娘

A Japanese
Folk Tale

Based on a Translation by
Teresa Peirce Williston

Illustrated by Dilleen Marsh

SILVERLEAF
PRESS

The Bamboo Princess

An old bamboo-cutter was going home through the shades of evening. Far away among the stalks of the feathery bamboo he saw a soft light. He went nearer to see what it was, and found it came from within one of the stalks.

He opened the bamboo stalk carefully, and found a tiny baby girl. She was only a few inches tall, but as beautiful as a fairy. Indeed he wondered if she were not really a fairy.

He carried her home to show his wife. They were very glad for they had no child, so they loved her as their own. In a few years she had grown to be a young woman. She was as sweet and kind as she was beautiful. A soft light always seemed to follow her.

They called her The Bamboo Princess, because she was found among the bamboo, and because she was more beautiful than any princess.

Far and wide, people heard of her beauty. Every day faces peeped through the hedge at the edge of the garden in hopes of seeing her.

Among those who came most often to the hedge were five princes. Each one thought The Bamboo Princess the most beautiful woman he had ever seen, and each wished her for his wife.

So each of the five wrote to the father of the princess asking to marry her. It so happened that all five letters were brought to the old man at the same time.

The old man did not know which one to choose, nor what to do. He was afraid, too, that if he chose one of the princes, the other four would be angry. But the princess had a plan. "Have them all come here," she said, "then we can choose more carefully."

On a certain day the
five princes came to
the house of the bamboo-cutter.
Each one thought he would be the
one she would marry. But the prin-
cess did not wish to marry any of them. She wanted stay with her dear
father and mother and take care of them as long as they lived. So she gave each
one something to do which was impossible.

The first she asked to go to India and find the great stone bowl of Buddha. The
second one was to bring her a branch from the jeweled trees that grew on the
floating mountain of Horai.

The third prince was asked to bring her a robe made from the skins of the fire
rats that grew more bright in flames. The fourth she told to bring a jewel from the
neck of the sea dragon, and the fifth she asked to bring her the shell which the
swallows keep hidden in their nests.

The princes hurried away, each anxious to be the first to return, and so marry
the beautiful Bamboo Princess.

The Great Stone Bowl

The prince who promised to go to India in search of the bowl was very lazy. When he found out that it would take three years to journey to India and back, he determined not to go.

Everyone told stories about a great bowl of Bhudda that gleamed and sparkled with beautiful gems. But the prince found a little stone bowl at a nearby temple and wrapped it in cloth of the richest silk. He made up a story about a fantastical trip to India, wrote it down and attached it to the box with the plain bowl inside. He waited three years before sending it to the princess.

But the princess was not fooled. When she read the letter she felt pity for the prince, but when she saw the common temple bowl in the box, she was angry and refused to admit the prince who came to call.

The prince felt sad, but he knew that he deserved it. He went back to his home but he kept the bowl to remind himself that you get nothing good in this world unless you work for it.

The Branch of the Jewel Tree

The prince who was going for the branch of the jewel tree was very cunning and very rich. He did not believe that there was a floating mountain called Horai. However, he said goodbye to all his friends and went down to the seashore. There he dismissed all but three of his servants, for he said he wished to go quietly. It was three years before anybody saw or heard of him again. Then he suddenly appeared before the princess, bearing a wonderful branch of gold with blossoms and leaves of all-colored jewels.

He told the princess of an ocean voyage filled with waves the size of mountains and strange sea creatures like dragon snakes. It was a wonderful story, but right in the middle three men came asking for the prince. "Could you pay us know?" they asked.

"Pay you for what?" the princess interrupted.

"For working to make this beautiful golden branch," they answered.

The prince was angry and ashamed. He knew that the princess would never believe in him again, so he went far away into another country to live.

The princess gave the jewel branch to the workmen to pay them, so they went away praising her for her kindness.

The Fire Robe

The third prince was to bring the robe made of the fur of the fire rats. He was very much loved and asked his friends all over the world to help him. No one had heard of it until, one day, one of his servants spoke up: "My lord," he said, "I remember hearing my grandfather tell about this fire robe. It was kept in a temple upon the top of a certain mountain, hundreds of miles from here."

The lord sent messengers to search out the temple. They searched for months and found nothing. Finally, they found a large iron box buried in the mountainside. Within it, wrapped in folds of silk was a beautiful fur robe.

"How beautiful the princess will look in this!" Prince Abe rejoiced. Then he remembered that fire rats' fur grew more bright in flames. "It cannot be too beautiful for the princess," he said.

He ordered a fire brought and laid the silver robe over the burning coals. Like a flash the red flames leaped up, and before he could snatch it from the fire there was nothing left but silvery smoke drifting off on the wind.

Prince Abe was heartbroken. He could only write to the princess telling her all, and then go away forever. When the princess heard of it, she wept. She sent for the prince but he had gone and was never heard of again.

The Shell in the Swallow's Nest

The prince who was to find the shell hid in the swallows' nest was a very proud and lordly man. He called his servants around him and demanded to know what they knew about swallows' nests, but no one had ever seen a shell. He asked his gardeners and his water carriers. At last he asked the children. One little boy thought he had seen a shell once up in the roof of the kitchen.

The prince was delighted and ordered his men to search the kitchen roof. They rigged up a rope and a basket so they could look into the nests. They searched and searched, but found no shell.

At last the prince grew impatient. He insisted on being pulled up himself. When he reached the nests the swallows began to peck at him. They did not care to have their eggs broken and their nests torn to pieces. They flew at him so furiously that they nearly pecked his eyes out.

"Help, help!" he screamed. The men began to lower the basket. Just then he remembered the shell and thrust his hand into a nest. There was something hard there. He seized it, but lost his balance and came tumbling down. In his hand he held a shell, it is true, but it was a bit of eggshell, and the egg was spattered all over his hand and face.

By the time his breaks and bruises were healed, he had forgotten all about the princess.

The Dragon Jewel

Prince Lofty was the one who was to bring the dragon jewel. He was a great boaster and a great coward. He did not doubt that he would win the princess, so he had a great palace built to receive her. All the wood was lacquered, carved, or inlaid with gold and precious stones. The walls were hung with silks painted by the finest artists.

He called together his servants and told them to fit up a boat. But when they learned they would go in search of a great dragon, the servants were fearful.

"Cowards!" cried Prince Lofty. "Learn how to be brave from me. Do you think I will be afraid of any dragon?" So they started, and all went well for three days.

Then a fierce storm came up. The boat rocked and great waves broke in foam over the side. Prince Lofty huddled in the bottom of the boat seasick and frightened. He begged the pilot to save him.

"What did you ever bring me to this place for?" he cried. "Did you wish to kill me? Is this all you care for the life of your great prince?"

When at last Prince Lofty felt firm ground under him he wept aloud and vowed he would never leave solid ground again. He was on an island far from Japan, but he would not return on a boat, not for a hundred princesses. The beautiful palace he built had no one to live in it but bats and owls.

The Smoke of Fuji Yama

Years passed by and the princess took good care of her old father and mother. They were very old now.

Now they saw why she had asked the five princes to do impossible things. She wanted to stay with her parents, and yet she knew that if she refused to marry, the princes they might be angry with her and harm her father.

Each day she grew more beautiful and more kind and gentle.

When she was twenty years old, which is quite old for a Japanese maiden, her mother died. Then she seemed to grow very sad. Whenever the full moon whitened the earth with its soft light, she would go away by herself and weep.

One evening late in summer she was sitting on a balcony looking up at the moon, and sobbing as though her heart would break.

Her old father came to her and said, "My daughter, tell me your trouble. I know that you have tried to keep it from me lest I should grieve, too, but it will kill me to see you so sad if I cannot help you."

Then the princess said, "I weep, dear Father, because I know that I must soon leave you. My home is really in the moon. I was sent here to take care of you, but now the time comes that I must go. When the next full moon comes, they will send for me."

Her father was sad indeed to hear this, but answered, "Do you think that I will let anyone come and take you away? I shall go to the Emperor himself and ask his aid."

Her father went to the Emperor and told him the whole story. The great Emperor was touched by the love of the maiden who had chosen to stay with her parents and care for them. He promised to send a whole army to guard the house when the time came. The old bamboo-cutter went home very cheerful, but the princess was sadder than ever.

The old moon faded away. A few nights showed only the blue of the heavens and the gold of the stars. Then a tiny silver thread showed just after sunset. Each night it widened and brightened. Each day the princess grew sadder and sadder.

The Emperor remembered his promise and sent a great army who camped about the house. Hundreds of men were placed on the roof of the house. Surely no one could enter through such a guard.

The first night of the full moon came. The princess waited on her balcony for the moon to rise.

Slowly over the tops of the trees on the mountain rose the great silver ball. Every sound was hushed.

The princess went to her father. He lay as if asleep. When she came near he opened his eyes. "I see now why you must go," he said. "It is because I am going, too. Thank you, my daughter, for all the happiness you have brought to us." Then he closed his eyes and she saw that he was dead.

The moon rose higher and higher. A line of light like a fairy bridge reached from heaven to earth.

Drifting down it, like smoke before the wind, came countless troops of soldiers in shining armor. There was no sound, no breath of wind, but on they came.

The soldiers of the Emperor stood as though turned to stone. The princess went forward to meet the leader of these heavenly visitors.

"I am ready," she said. There was no other sound. Silently he handed her a tiny cup. Just as silently she drank from it. It was the water of forgetfulness. All her life on earth faded from her. Once more she was a moon maiden and would live forever.

The leader gently laid a mantle of gleaming snow-white feathers over her shoulders. Her old garments slipped to the earth and disappeared.

Rising like the morning mists that lie along the lake, the heavenly company passed slowly to the top of Fuji Yama, the sacred mountain of Japan.

On, on, up through the still whiteness of the moonlight, the long line passed, until once more they reached the silver gates of the moon city, where all is happiness and peace.

Men say that even now a soft white wreath of smoke curls up from the sacred crown of Fuji Yama, like a floating bridge to that fair city far off in the sky....

Notes from the Illustrator

My husband's grandfather served in World War II. Among his wartime souvenirs was an accordion-style book of Japanese block prints. This depiction of Japanese stories was passed down to us and became my primary reference for fabric and style designs in *The Bamboo Cutter and the Moon Maiden.*

Bamboo Borders

I chose a different bamboo border for the panels depicting each of the prince's adventures. The personal character of each prince suggested the particular bamboo:

The prince sent to find the great stone bowl of Buddha was *lazy*. His border of bamboo resembles lifeless bones and the leaves are wilted. When bamboo has closed its leaves through drought, it must be watered within a matter of hours, or it will die. Once the leaf cells are damaged they will not be able to take in water and swell again. The neglected state of this bamboo reflects the lazy prince's inattention to his duty to the princess.

The prince sent to procure a branch from the jewel tree was a *liar*. The bamboo representing him is the *Great Thorned Bamboo* (shown here). Thick, unrefined, and full of thorns, this bamboo is dangerous to all who touch it carelessly.

The prince sent by the princess to bring the fire robe was an honorable man but he was *foolish*. For Prince Abe, I painted the *Arrow Bamboo*. This bamboo is straight and true and is also less invasive than many other running bamboos. But I painted it thin and immature. Like the light green shoots of an immature plant, Prince Abe couldn't bear the weight of his mistake and went away forever.

The prince sent to find the shell in the swallow's nest was *angry* and cruel. He is represented by a border of early shoots of *Shimofuri Bamboo*. This is a vigorous species and needs much effort to keep it both looking good and under control. This prince's lack of control only won him cuts and bruises.

Prince Lofty was a *coward* hiding behind great boasting. His bamboo border is of fattened bamboo internodes swollen with water. Waterlogged bamboo can look strong, but it is weak and susceptible to infectious fungi.

The Illustration Process

These illustrations are of mixed media. The preliminary drawings were traced onto watercolor paper with a brush line of gray acrylic paint. Black areas were penned and painted with permanent black India ink. White or light areas were painted with Art Masking Fluid. The paper was then stretched taut on a drawing board with dampened brown packing tape. Each illustration was given a wash with acrylic paint in a different combination of background colors. After drying, the masked areas were cleaned off with an eraser. Details were painted with acrylic paint using a fine brush. Highlights and glows were created using Prismacolor pencils on top of the acrylics. Pelikan Graphic White painted with a *very* tiny brush created the whitest finishing touches and highlights.